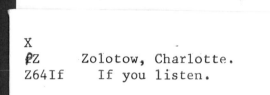

IF YOU LISTEN

An Ursula Nordstrom Book

IF YOU LISTEN

Charlotte Zolotow

Illustrations by Marc Simont

Harper & Row, Publishers

Library of Congress Cataloging in Publication Data
Zolotow, Charlotte Shapiro, date
    If you listen.

    "An Ursula Nordstrom book."
    SUMMARY: A mother reassures her little girl
there is a way to know that someone far away loves
you.
    [1. Love—Fiction]   I. Simont, Marc.
II. Title.
PZ7.Z77Ih   1980   [E]   79-2688
ISBN 0-06-027049-7
ISBN 0-06-027050-0 lib. bdg.

IF YOU LISTEN

The little girl's father had been away
a long time.
"How do you know if someone far away
is loving you?" she asked.
"Do you mean your father?"
her mother said, smiling.
"Yes," said the little girl. "If I can't
see him, or hear him, or feel his hugs,
how can I know he loves me
when he isn't here?"

"You have to stop when you're lonely and listen," said her mother.

"Listen the way you do when
you can't see the church steeple,
but suddenly the sound of bells
comes through the air to you.
If you listen hard enough
you almost hear the song they play.

"Or," said her mother, "it's like
lying in bed at night and all you see
is the darkness of your bedroom around you,
but you feel the night outside too,
reaching away into the distance,

and you hear the sound of a foghorn
from a river miles away

or a dog barking somewhere in the hills

"Or," her mother went on, "it's like
staring at the mountains
on a hot summer day and nothing is moving,
not a leaf or a bird or a blade of grass,

when suddenly a flash of lightning
streaks across the sky
and you hear the thunder behind it
coming close.

Or you're sitting alone in the living room
not thinking of anything at all
and one petal falls off a rose
in the vase on the coffee table,

or outside in the orchard one apple
suddenly falls off the apple tree
and makes a thump near you in the grass.

"You have to listen inside yourself,"
her mother said,
"just the way you strain
to hear the dog barking in the hills,
or the train rushing by in the night,

or the rustle of birds
in the leaves of the trees,
or the church bells
from a church you can't see,
or a boat whistle in the fog.
If you listen hard you'll feel
someone far away sending love to you."

The little girl sat still a long time.
She was thinking of her father.
She looked up at the sky.
It was a clear blue. One bird
circled and circled overhead.
She watched until he flew away.

Then she came over and put her head
in her mother's lap.
And her mother brushed the hair back
from the little girl's face.
"I will listen hard,"
the little girl said,
"but I wish he'd come home."